MESSENGER P.L. OF NORTH AURORA
3 6878 00128 584
P9-DDF-345

Haunted Castle Tour

Spooky!

At Weasel Towers tonight...

Watch out!
Weasel in ghost costume about!

HUNGRY CROCS IN THE MOAT

£20

...e
...fic
experiment. Must have an interest in cheese. Apply to Rat's laboratory.
0356713

FAT CAT

Wants new home/owner, preferably with large swimming pool.
Only eats caviar from a silver dish.
Call Mr Tibbles: 06571-287

S. Weasel: If you are reading this, I want an apology.
Shrew.

MISSING

4 large, dangerous crocodiles, stolen from the safari park 2 weeks ago. If found do not panic – call Stan's Safari Park.

WEASEL'S AUTOS

Every car is guaranteed to break down as soon as you leave my garage!

USED CARS

MAKE A FORTUNE
from others' Misfortune!

EAT AT WEASEL BURGER

Unhealthy food, terrible service!

COUPON

This book belongs to:

Sneaky Weasel ESQ

and

KEEP OFF!

THIS IS A BORZOI BOOK PUBLISHED BY ALFRED A. KNOPF
Copyright © 2008 by Hannah Shaw

All rights reserved. Published in the United States by Alfred A. Knopf,
an imprint of Random House Children's Books,
a division of Random House, Inc., New York.

Originally published in Great Britain in 2008 by Jonathan Cape, an imprint of Random House Children's Books.

Knopf, Borzoi Books, and the colophon are registered trademarks of Random House, Inc.

Visit us on the Web! www.randomhouse.com/kids

Educators and librarians, for a variety of teaching tools,
visit us at www.randomhouse.com/teachers

Library of Congress Cataloging-in-Publication Data is available on request.

ISBN 978-0-375-85625-9 (trade) ISBN 978-0-375-95625-6 (lib. bdg.)

The illustrations in this book were created using a combination of pen and ink, printmaking techniques, and Photoshop.

MANUFACTURED IN MALAYSIA
February 2009
10 9 8 7 6 5 4 3 2 1

First American Edition

Random House Children's Books supports the First Amendment and celebrates the right to read.

Sneaky Weasel

Hannah Shaw

ALFRED A. KNOPF NEW YORK

Weasel was sneaky.

He was a bully and a cheat
– a nasty, measly Weasel.

His *mean* schemes and *cunning* tricks
had made him *richer* than
you can possibly imagine.

New!
GHASTLY GREASY GRUB AT WEASEL BURGER
WEASEL TOWERS KEEP OUT!

One day Weasel decided to throw a party to boast about his incredible castle, fast car and huge swimming pool.
He sent off invitations to everyone he could think of.
S W
invitation
Dear friends,
I, Sneaky Weasel, invite you –
yes, you – to a party.
I am very rich and important,
so don't be late.
Signed,
S. Weasel ESQ
S. Weasel ESQ. at Weasel Towers
P.S. Watch out, the crocodiles in the moat might be hungry!
1st
Rat

W
W
On the day of the party
Weasel dressed in his finest clothes
and admired himself in the mirror.
"Don't I look handsome?"
he asked his reflection.

Then Weasel waited expectantly for his guests to arrive.

He waited...

and Waited...

But no one came.

Being rich and powerful isn't much fun when there's no one to impress.

"Why would anyone not want to come to my party?"
sulked Weasel.
"I will visit them all and demand an explanation."

First, Weasel went to see Rabbit. He banged on the door.
When Rabbit saw Weasel, he started shaking.
"What's the matter with you?" said Weasel crossly.
"And why didn't you come to my party?"

Rabbit looked a bit *upset*.
"Don't you remember how **mean** to me you were at school?" he asked.
"Oh," said Weasel, *re*membering.
MR MOLE
SW! RULES!
Raddit pie

Next, Weasel went to see Rat in his *laboratory*.
"Why didn't you come to my party?"
he snapped.

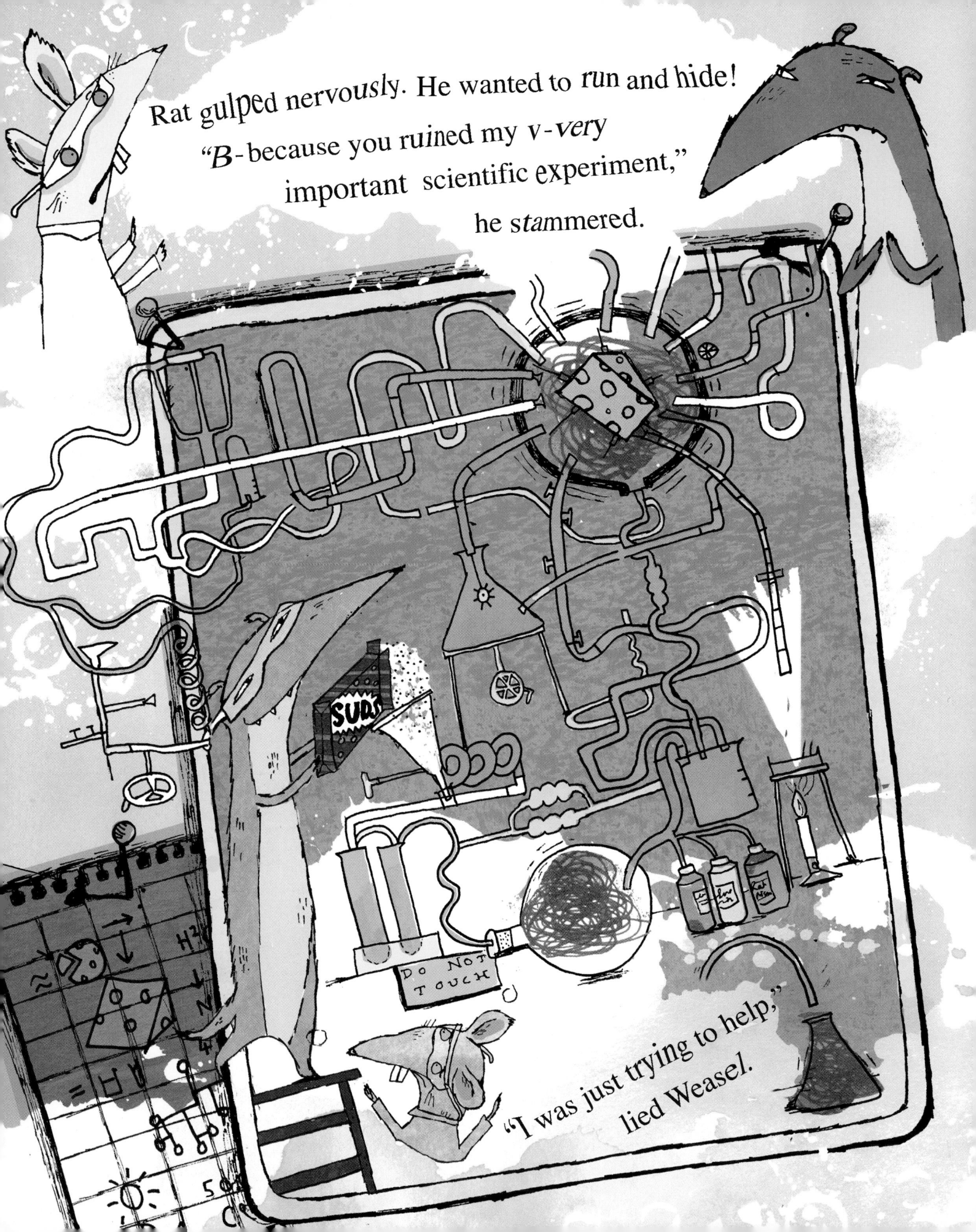
Rat gulped nervously. He wanted to run and hide!
"B-because you ruined my v-very important scientific experiment," he stammered.
SUDS
DO NOT TOUCH
"I was just trying to help," lied Weasel.

Off Weasel went to visit Hedgehog,
but on the way he met Hedgehog's mum.
"Hedgehog isn't *very* well," she said.

"He's been scratching for days and days and he just can't stop."

"Ah," said Weasel, feeling a bit itchy himself.

Weasel was starting to feel quite *guilty,*
so he *crept* past Shrew's house.
"Not so *fast,*" said a little voice.
Shrew
Recycling
RECYCLE MORE!

"It was a joke," protested Weasel.
"My cat only likes caviar,
he wouldn't eat you."

"Well it wasn't funny," squeaked Shrew.

"Nobody came to your party because
you're mean and nasty and a bad friend.
And you never ever say sorry!"

Weasel went *home* feeling m*easly*.
He had been a *horrible bully*.
"I *must find* a way to be a *good* friend,"
he thought desperately,
"but h*ow?*"

Weasel paced round and round all night,
trying to think of good ideas.
This wasn't easy because
most of his thoughts were *wickedly* sneaky,
but by morning he had a plan . . .

"What *I* need to do," said Weasel,
"is put right everything I've done wrong."
So that is *exactly* what he did.

Everyone was pleased that Weasel was making *such* an effort.

"But there is still one thing we *hav*en't heard you say," said Shrew.

Weasel thought long and hard. After a while, he began to mumble,

"I'm *so* . . . *so* important! No . . . I'm *su* . . . super sneaky?"

The other animals began to laugh.

"I've got *it!*" cried Weasel.

"I'm sorry!"

"Hurray!" they all cheered.

Weasel decided to throw a party
to celebrate being good at being good.

SORRY!
HEDGEHOG
FREE MONEY
WEASEL DELI
RABBIT
RAT
WEASEL says FRIENDS ARE VERY IMPORTANT
invitation
Dear friends,
Please come to my party.
There will be jelly, cake and ice cream and I will be on my best behavior.
Yours sincerely-ish,
Weasel
PS. Don't worry, the crocodiles in the moat have been sent back to the safari park.

This time, everyone came.

"Yippee!" cried Weasel.

"Let's party!"

Choc
So Good

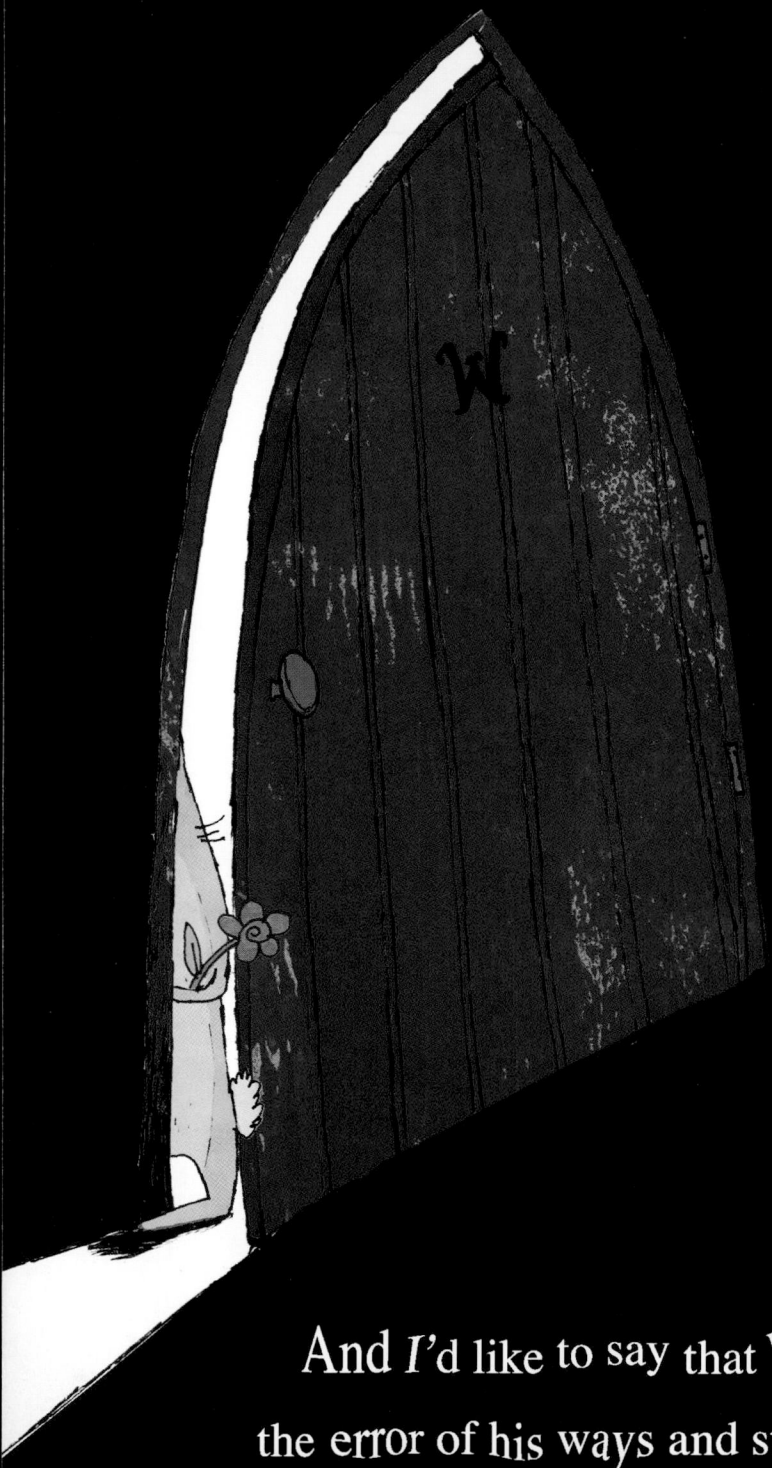

And *I*'d like to say that Weasel *finally* learned
the error of his ways and stopped being sneaky altogether.

But *sometimes* he just couldn't help himself . . .

So Good

NEW from Weasel PRODUCTS LTD.

Weasel Teddy
Give me a cuddle!

Instant Fur
For those who like the fluffy look!

Happy like Weasel
Fun-to-wear T-shirt

CALL THE SALES NO: 0979931

EVERYONE NEEDS

Flowers

Tickets for a day out

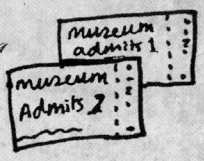

Weasel's Nice Surprise kit!

Non-Exploding Cake

Happy Snapshot Camera

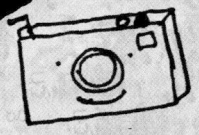

Thank-you Card

Nice-flavoured sweets

Let your friends know you CARE

FREE MONEY & PIGGY BANK

WEASEL BANK

Money will not be kept in a swimming pool.

ANTI-FLEA SHAMPOO

Gets rid of even the toughest fleas!

Banish fleas!